THE PURRFECT DAY

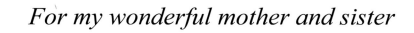

For my wonderful mother and sister

KITTY CONES

THE PURRFECT DAY

WRITTEN AND ILLUSTRATED BY
RALPH COSENTINO

INSIGHT KIDS
San Rafael, California

In a small town by the bay,
above the best ice cream parlor in town,
lived three sweet little kitties.

They each loved ice cream!
Koko always chose yummy chocolate.
Yumi had to have sweet vanilla.
Miyu couldn't get enough tasty strawberry.

It had rained all week, but today the sun was shining!
The three best friends couldn't wait to play outside.
Mew, mew! What could they do?

Yumi looked for ideas,
while Koko tried playing tag with Miyu.
Miyu just wished she were **far away**.
Mew, mew! Yumi knew just what to do!

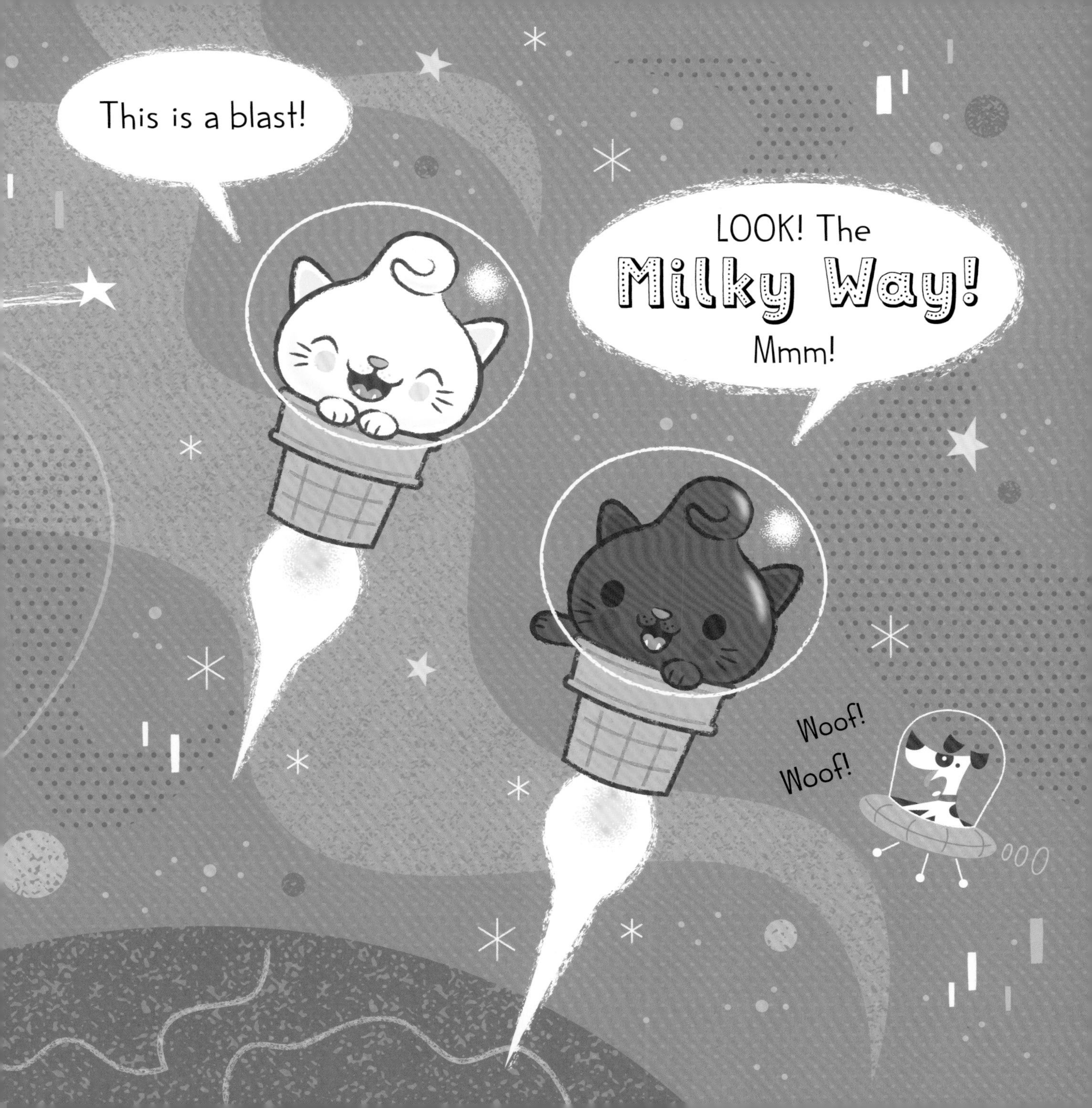
This is a blast!
LOOK! The Milky Way! Mmm!
Woof! Woof!
ooo

But flying through space made Miyu's head spin.
And seeing the Milky Way made them all hungry!
Mew, mew! Yumi knew just what to do!

Soon, they were bobbing in the bay, fishing for breakfast!

But it was a windy day. A giant wave came rumbling toward Miyu just as her fishing line broke.

Getting wet was not Miyu's idea of fun.

Her friends tried to cheer her up with sprinkles.
She wasn't **amused**.
Mew, mew! Koko knew just what to do!

What better place to have fun than the **amusement** park?

But roller coasters made poor Miyu's stomach queasy.

She needed some fresh **air**.
Mew, mew! Yumi knew just what to do!

They could fly **hot air** balloons!

Miyu was so embarrassed that
she wanted to **hide** under a rock.
Mew, mew! Koko knew just what to do!

They could play **hide**-and-go-seek!

Miyu looked and looked, but she couldn't
find Yumi or Koko. It was getting late,
and she was scared of the dark.

Miyu missed her friends.
She didn't want to play outside anymore.

Yumi and Koko ran to her side.
Mew, mew! This time, Miyu knew just what to do!

So they rushed home, straight into Miyu's room!

They read comics, played games,
ate ice cream, and had a great time.

Just being together made it a perfect day after all.

Mew, mew! They all knew just what to do.
As the stars twinkled and the moon shone bright, Koko,
Miyu, and Yumi snuggled close and said good night.

The end.

INSIGHT
K I D S

An Imprint of Insight Editions
PO Box 3088
San Rafael, CA 94912
www.insighteditions.com

Find us on Facebook: www.facebook.com/InsightEditions
Follow us on Twitter: @insighteditions

Library of Congress Cataloging-in-Publication Data available.

ISBN: 978-1-68383-239-3

Publisher: Raoul Goff
Associate Publisher: Jon Goodspeed
Art Director: Chrissy Kwasnik
Designers: Ralph Cosentino and Lauren Chang
Associate Editor: Erum Khan
Managing Editor: Alan Kaplan
Production Editor: Lauren LePera
Associate Production Manager: Sam Taylor

Insight Editions, in association with Roots of Peace, will plant two trees for each tree used in the
manufacturing of this book. Roots of Peace is an internationally renowned humanitarian organization
dedicated to eradicating land mines worldwide and converting war-torn lands into productive farms
and wildlife habitats. Roots of Peace will plant two million fruit and nut trees in Afghanistan and provide
farmers there with the skills and support necessary for sustainable land use.

Printed in China by C&C Offset Printing Co., Ltd.

10 9 8 7 6 5 4 3 2 1